DISASTER STRIKES

Earthquake Shock

DON'T MISS A MINUTE OF THESE HEART-STOPPING ADVENTURES!

Earthquake Shock

Tornado Alley

DISASTER STRIKES

Earthquake Shock

by **MARLANE KENNEDY**

illustrated by
ERWIN MADRID

SCHOLASTIC INC.

No part of this publication may be reproduced, stored in a retrieval system, or transmitted in any form or by any means, electronic, mechanical, photocopying, recording, or otherwise, without written permission of the publisher. For information regarding permission, write to Scholastic Inc., Attention: Permissions Department, 557 Broadway, New York, NY 10012.

ISBN 978-0-545-53044-6

12 11 10 9 8 7 6 5 4   14 15 16 17 18 19/0

Printed in the U.S.A.   40
First printing, January 2014

Designed by Nina Goffi

For Jenne Abramowitz and Lauren Tarshis, my two fairy godsisters for the Disaster Strikes series. You each shook up my world as an author and I am forever grateful!

CHAPTER 1

Ten-year-old Joey Flores stood on top of the ramp. He took a deep breath, adjusted the strap to his helmet, and motioned to his friend Kevin Chen to begin filming.

He pushed off on his skateboard, and when he'd gained enough speed, ollied up onto the foot-high railing. He slid sideways on the rail, down the entire length of the ramp, then popped off the end, knees bent, landing with a satisfying clatter and pumping his fist in the air. "Did you catch that?" he yelled to Kevin. Joey had gotten the skateboard for his last birthday, and even though he spent all his free time at the skate park, with its half-pipes, railings, ramps, and jumps, this was the first time he'd actually landed this trick without falling.

Kevin grinned and gave a thumbs-up, while Joey's other friend Fiona Rollins slapped him on the back as she skated past him on her board.

It was the perfect moment.

Until . . .

"Woo-hoo, way to go, honey!"

Joey's mother waved at him from the grassy area at the edge of the park. In front of her, his baby sister, Allie, sat in her stroller, chewing and drooling on a rubbery teething ring.

"Yes, way to go, honnnn-*ney*," Dylan Jones whispered, sneering at Joey as he skated by.

Dylan lived in the same apartment complex as Joey and had a habit of giving him a hard time ever since . . . well . . . ever since Joey could remember. Dylan's mother was good friends with Joey's mother, which meant that even though Dylan was two years older than Joey, their moms often forced them to spend time together. When they were little, Dylan would take Joey's toys from him. Then as Dylan grew older he learned to tease. He wasn't really a bully; he was more like an annoying big brother, as hard to ignore as a pesky giant mosquito. Right now Joey was trying his best to pretend he didn't hear Dylan, but, man, was he steamed!

Joey also tried his best to avoid eye contact with his mother. The skate park was only about a fifteen-minute walk from his house. All the other neighborhood kids could hang out without some worried adult hovering over them. Unfortunately, Joey's mom thought he was too young to be left at the park unattended. It was totally embarrassing.

But a beautiful afternoon awaited him, so instead of getting upset with his over-protective mom, Joey focused on the fact that it was 4:30 on a Friday. The school week was over, and he was at his favorite place in the world: the skate park. Plus the sun was shining, the sky was blue, it wasn't too warm or too cold — just the perfect spring day in his neighborhood, located on the outskirts of downtown Los Angeles.

Now that he'd mastered the foot-high rail, it was time to move on and try some new tricks. He was on a hot streak, he could feel it. Maybe he would even try to drop in off the half-pipe!

Joey skated over to it and found Fiona was already curving her board up and down the rounded sides. She flew up and held her board still for a moment on the top edge, then glided back down effortlessly.

Kevin was filming her every movement with his handheld cam. Kevin wanted to be a filmmaker when he grew up. He saw the world through a lens, and capturing the action at the skate park was good practice. He would take home what he shot and upload it onto his computer. Then he'd edit it, put it to music, and add special effects.

Joey was impressed that Kevin could make even him look good. Joey hadn't been skateboarding that long, but his friend made him look almost like a pro.

He had a long way to go to be as good as Fiona, though. Even without Kevin's fancy editing, she was amazing. She had been skateboarding since she was four. Her dad used to be a competitive skateboarder, so she got an early start. Now her dad was a graphic designer and artist. But every once in a while he would stop by the park and wow everyone. He could even do a flip off the half-pipe! He was really cool . . . for a dad.

Joey's dad was an accountant. It had to be the most boring job in the world. He was a nice guy and all, but he dressed, well, like a dad. Fiona's dad sort of looked like a rock star.

Fiona finally came to a stop, and Joey

tried to gather his courage. He'd never gone down the half-pipe from the top edge before, but he felt like today would be the day. So he flipped his board up and caught it, then started walking toward the stairs that lead to the top.

But he was stopped cold in his tracks.

"Joey, sweetie," his mother yelled. "We need to go! I forgot to bring an extra diaper, and Allie needs to be changed!"

The park was suddenly silent, and it felt like every single eye was on him. Then some boy laughed, and soon lots of kids joined in. Joey just wanted to melt into the ground and disappear.

But his embarrassment quickly became aggravation. Skateboard in hand, he ran over to where his mom stood. "We just got here," he complained. "You said we could stay for an hour."

"I know. And I'm sorry. I thought there were extra diapers in the diaper bag, but there aren't. And now your little sister really stinks."

Joey eyed his sister and tried not to breathe in too deeply. The whole situation stunk in more ways than one.

His sister looked up at him, grinned, and wrinkled her nose.

"Look at her. She doesn't mind," Joey said. "She's not crying or anything."

"I am not going to have her sit in a dirty diaper while you skate," his mom said, her voice firm.

"Then just go home. Let me skate for another half hour. I can walk home after I'm done."

His mother sighed. "I've been over this with you before. You are not old enough to be on your own here. Maybe in a few years, but not now."

Dylan came rattling over on his skateboard, jumping off as it hit the grassy area. "I can walk Joey home," he offered.

Mrs. Flores hesitated. She cocked an eyebrow and looked at Dylan uncertainly.

"I have to be home in time for dinner anyway, so I'll have him back by five thirty," Dylan said.

"Well . . . if you'll be leaving that soon . . . I guess it will be fine." Her expression relaxed a bit and she smiled. "Kids your age often babysit, don't they?"

Joey rolled his eyes. How could his mom think he needed to be babysat? And by Dylan of all people! But if it meant he could skate longer, he wasn't about to complain.

"Thanks, Dylan." Mrs. Flores pushed the stroller toward the sidewalk and called over her shoulder. "Be careful, Joey. And don't try any new tricks, okay?"

"Okay," Joey said. But he'd already decided that as soon as she was out of sight, he'd make a beeline for the top of the half-pipe.

As he walked back toward the concrete skating area, Dylan said in a sickening singsong voice, "Be careful Joey-Woey. You might get a boo-boo. And Mommy won't be here to make it all better." He laughed and his voice became deep. "And I ain't about to kiss no scraped knee!"

Minutes later, Joey was poised on the edge of the half-pipe. Most of his board dangled in the air, his left foot was planted on the back to steady him. Kevin had his camcorder pointed at him, ready to capture his first-time plunge in all its glory.

Joey was nervous. It was a loooooong way down.

"Chicken!" Dylan called out. *"Bawk, bawk, bawk.* You don't have the guts!"

All at once, Joey stomped on the front of his board, setting the inevitable ride in motion.

Whoa! He had never gone this fast before. He sped toward the bottom of the half-pipe, but suddenly fell off the board sideways. His board reached the bottom without him, and he trailed, careening feet-first, as if flying down a playground slide.

Dylan was laughing his head off. "What was that?"

Fiona shot Dylan a look. "Like I've never seen you do that," she said. "That was an excellent first try," she told Joey. "You got more than halfway down!"

Despite the failure, Joey felt a surge of excitement as he leapt to his feet. He had wanted to try dropping down the half-pipe since he first got his board, and he finally had. It wasn't nearly as scary as he'd thought it would be.

And by the time Dylan was supposed to walk him home, Joey had finally made it all the way down and sailed up the other side without falling.

CHAPTER 2

Joey couldn't wait the day or two it would take for Kevin to do his video magic. Kevin had filmed his successful glide along the ramp rail and his half-pipe plunge and also some really cool tricks Fiona did, so they wanted to watch the rough video at Joey's right away.

Joey's mom thought he was too young for a cell phone, so he'd borrowed Kevin's to ask her if it was okay, and his mom had invited both his friends to stay for Friday night pizza. She'd invited Dylan, too, but when Joey mentioned it, Dylan snickered. "Like I would want to hang out with a bunch of little kids. Get real."

As the group skated along a stretch of sidewalk, Dylan continued to give Joey a hard time. That was probably why he volunteered to walk him home, Joey figured.

"Did you know when Joey was five he got sick at his birthday party and threw up on his birthday cake? He blew out the candles and then blew chunks." Dylan laughed, amused at his own joke.

Kevin noticed Joey's perturbed scowl and quickly changed the subject. "It would be neat to film you doing a kickflip along the sidewalk," he told Dylan. "I could put together a clip with a slow-motion effect to see the board turning and rotating in the air."

Dylan thought that was a great idea. He liked showing off. The two lagged behind for a moment to set things up, while Fiona and Joey zipped ahead toward a large concrete overpass. Their neighborhood lay on the other side of the highway, past the grassy hillside planted with flowers. Next came a cluster of tidy bungalow houses, and beyond that, the apartment complex where Joey and Dylan lived.

The sidewalk continued underneath the arched tunnel, and soon Joey and Fiona were in the shade it provided as cars hummed overhead. It was the beginning of rush hour and a steady line of cars drove on the road alongside them, the noise echoing under the highway.

All at once, Joey heard an earsplitting boom. A jolt knocked him forward and he stumbled off his board. He glanced over at Fiona. She was still on her board, but she looked as if she'd felt the jolt, too. Had a car run into the wall behind them? As he turned to look, the sidewalk shifted under his feet. He tried to keep his balance, but the sidewalk began to roll like a fun-house floor. Joey heard an awful rumbling and the sound of cracking concrete, and suddenly he knew exactly what was happening.

It was an earthquake. Joey had lived through several minor ones, but this one felt different. They had to get out from underneath the highway.

Fiona had jumped off her board now, but she stood paralyzed. Joey grabbed her arm, yanking her. "You have to run," he shouted. "Now!"

Her voice trembled. "I d-don't know if I c-can."

"You have to!" Joey yelled as he dragged her forward.

But it was nearly impossible to run with the ground rising and falling every which way. They both fell several times and had to keep dragging each other back up as small chunks of concrete and dust rained down from above.

The sun, oblivious to the earthquake, was cheerfully beating down only a few feet away. "Just a little farther," Joey screamed at Fiona. They lurched forward, holding hands. Crashing concrete columns chased them, like some awful monster ready to swallow them whole. "Ow!" Something hard and heavy slammed into Joey's shoulder. But they couldn't afford to stop moving.

Finally the ground quieted long enough

for Joey and Fiona to reach the patch of sunlight they'd seen. But before they could get much farther, the ground pitched violently again and they were surrounded by a deafening explosion — the sickening sound of total collapse.

Fiona tripped, bringing Joey down with her. He fell so hard the air was knocked out of his lungs. He couldn't breathe. He couldn't move. The ground jerked in fits under his body, while the thunderous groans and shrieks of the highway overpass tumbling down grew quieter. The ground gave one last exhausted shudder. Joey lay still, trying to get his deflated lungs to fill with air.

After what seemed to be an eternity he sucked in a breath and sat up. It took him a moment to realize he was okay. His knees were scraped and bleeding. His shoulder throbbed. He tenderly touched where it had been struck. Whatever had pelted him had left one heck of a bruise. He looked over at Fiona. She lay in a limp heap on the ground, surrounded by small pieces of rubble and a fine coating of dust. Her eyes were wide open and she had a shocked look on her face.

"Fiona?" he said. He gently touched her arm. "Are you okay?"

She didn't respond.

CHAPTER 3

For a terrible moment Joey thought Fiona was dead. But then she blinked and coughed. She slowly pulled herself into a sitting position. "I'm okay . . . I think." She touched her forehead where a large purple goose egg was forming. "I must look terrible," she said.

Silly with relief, Joey felt like laughing. Fiona had been through an earthquake, had a huge knot in the middle of her forehead, and she was worried about how she looked!

But his spirits quickly sank as the scope of what had just happened dawned on him.

There were cracks not only in the sidewalk, but in the road that lay in front of them. In fact, a huge one split the pavement just yards away from where he'd fallen. It was at least a foot or two deep. Large chunks of the sidewalk and road jutted upright in the air. The cars that had zipped by moments earlier were now tossed about, their drivers and passengers shaken and stunned. Joey could see a house up ahead in partial collapse. Windows shattered. Walls crumbling.

Slowly, Joey and Fiona turned, looking

in the direction they had just come from. Only a few feet away the rubble was thick and deep with enormous concrete slabs rising at odd angles — a small mountain before them. Three cars had fallen when the overpass collapsed. One lay on its side, crumpled by the impact. Another rested nose down, the hood hidden by debris. The third, miraculously undamaged, sat at the very top of the heap of concrete, balanced on a fairly level portion of road that had fallen in one piece.

But what lay underneath? Joey and Fiona had left their skateboards behind. His skateboard was his prized possession, but now thinking about what else might be buried, it didn't seem all that important.

How could the world change so drastically in such a short time? One moment everything was normal and the next . . .

All at once, his thoughts flashed to his friends. A sick feeling invaded the pit of his stomach. Kevin! Dylan! What had happened to them?

Joey looked at Fiona. By the panicked look in her eyes, he knew she was thinking the same thing. "How far behind were they?" she asked.

Joey shrugged. "I'm not sure. I wasn't really paying attention, but they had to have been close."

His thoughts turned to his mother and Allie. They would have been home at the time the earthquake struck. Their apartment was on the third floor of the complex. What if the building had collapsed just like the overpass?

A wave of shame overtook Joey. How could he have been so embarrassed to have them around earlier? If only they were safe, he thought, he wouldn't care if they watched over him at the skate park until he was thirty!

And his father had probably been on his way home from work when the earthquake struck. It was a long drive. How many overpasses were between here and his dad's office? He had no idea.

It didn't matter that his father was a boring accountant. It didn't matter that he wasn't cool, with long hair and ripped jeans. He was the best father in the world. Joey ached to be home on a normal day, to see his dad in his business suit and tie, coming through the door of the apartment as always, scooping up Allie, kissing his mom, and giving him a hug or ruffling his hair.

Fiona must have been having similar thoughts. She was crying, but managed to force out a few words. "What do we do now?"

By this time drivers were getting out of their cars. And people from damaged houses were streaming outside, filling the area. Some were walking around like expressionless zombies, but others were springing into action, helping those with obvious injuries. Two brave men and a courageous woman climbed the concrete heap toward the crumpled cars stuck in the jumbled remains of the overpass to check for injured passengers.

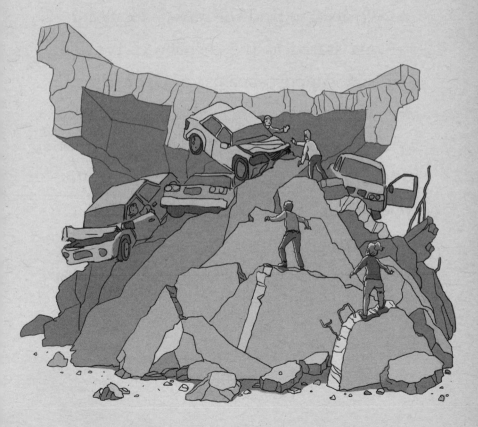

Even if his family needed help, they were too far away for him to do anything for them right now. But Kevin and Dylan — they had to be nearby. And no one else would know where to look for them.

"We need to find the guys," Joey said.

Fiona stared at the carnage of twisted steel-rod support beams and shuddered. Her hand flew to her mouth, as if she were trying to stuff her emotions back inside herself. She took a jagged breath, collected herself, and nodded.

It might be impossible to locate Kevin and Dylan, but Joey knew they had to try.

CHAPTER 4

"Let's go." Fiona immediately began to climb the jumbled heap of concrete, making a beeline to the other side.

As he watched her try to find footing on the pile of jagged debris, something occurred to Joey. "Fiona, wait! What if there's an aftershock? Don't climb that thing — it could crumble. It'll be safer to go around." He pointed at the grassy hillside, where colorful yellow and red flowers stood up straight, undamaged and beautiful. There had been nothing above to fall and crush them. Only the bright blue sky.

"Dylan!" Fiona yelled as she and Joey climbed the hillside as quickly as they could manage. "Kevin! Are you there?"

When they reached the top, they peered down the other side, frantically scanning the area for any sight of their friends. But all they saw was more rubble and smashed cars. That and the panicked faces of people with broken arms and bleeding cuts, struggling to make sense of what had just happened. The faces were all unfamiliar.

The two picked their way down the hillside. Fiona cupped her hands around her mouth once more and shouted, "Kevin! Dylan!"

There was no answer.

"I don't think they made it out in time like we did. They couldn't have. Finding them will be impossible." Fiona's voice  sounded frail and broken. Her face looked white, as if the reality of the situation had drained the color from her skin. "What are we going to tell their families?"

Joey felt a growing sense of dread. A bloodied man who'd just been pulled from his car stumbled toward them and Joey shuddered. He wanted to run away from it all. But he couldn't do it. He couldn't leave his friends behind.

"No. They *are* around here. Somewhere. We just have to find them," he announced. And even though he didn't want to, he took a few more steps toward the wreckage, with Fiona trailing close behind.

It was then that he heard it. "*Uhhhhng.*" A faint groan slipped out from under several large concrete slabs. Fiona grabbed his arm and pointed. She'd heard it, too. "Someone's trapped in there."

Joey could tell the slabs would be too

heavy to lift. But when he looked more closely, he saw an opening where the slabs leaned against each other. He was afraid to peek into the dark opening. Afraid of what he might see. But he knelt down anyway, his knees pressing against sharp shards of rubble, and cocked his head.

Joey couldn't believe his eyes. It was Dylan!

The older boy lay on his stomach, holding his cell phone to his ear. "*Uhhhng!*" he groaned again. It seemed more a groan of frustration than one of pain. Suddenly, he noticed Joey and a big relieved look took over his face. "Boy, am I glad to see you! My leg is trapped, and I'm kind of freaking out! I was trying to call for help, but I can't get through anywhere. I think the lines are jammed."

Fiona dropped down beside Joey and peered into the opening, too. "Dylan! Thank goodness! Are you okay?"

He nodded. "I think so," he said slowly. Then he frowned. "My leg doesn't hurt. At least not much — I just can't seem to move it. I'm stuck. You guys gotta do something, man."

Joey hadn't thought he would ever feel

happy to see Dylan. But he was. Sure, Dylan pestered and teased, but he was a part of Joey's life. And had been for a long time.

All at once, Joey felt strange vibrations under his knees. He heard a scream in the distance. The concrete slabs covering Dylan trembled and threatened to fall in. Dylan lashed out with his hands. "Get me out of here!" he yelled.

"We're coming!" Fiona cried. She and Joey reached under the concrete and grabbed Dylan's arms. They braced themselves and pulled with all their strength, straining and grunting as they worked to yank him free. Dylan did not budge.

When the ground finally grew quiet, Joey and Fiona released their grasp on

Dylan. The aftershock hadn't lasted long. But Joey knew a stronger one could come along at any moment. They had to get Dylan out now! Joey surveyed the situation. The slabs that trapped his friend were really heavy and propping each other up. So even if he and Fiona could manage to lift one, it would cause the other to come crashing down. If only Joey could see exactly how Dylan was pinned beneath them, maybe he could come up with a plan.

"Give me your phone," Joey said.

"That won't help. I already told you the lines are jammed," Dylan grumbled.

"I need it for the light. I'm going to try to crawl in beside you — headfirst — maybe I can figure out why you're stuck."

"You can't do that!" Fiona said. "What if there is another aftershock while you're in there? Those two pieces of concrete must weigh hundreds of pounds at least. If they fell . . ." She winced at the gruesome thought.

But that was a risk Joey had to take. He reached in and took Dylan's phone from him, then lay on the ground and soldier-crawled into the tunnel, digging his elbows into the rough debris as he inched along. It was a tight fit. And as the space narrowed, it became darker. He lit up the cell phone screen and turned it toward Dylan's leg. Joey ran his hand along Dylan's leg, but couldn't figure out what was trapping him under the rubble.

"His leg looks fine," Joey called. But as he shined the light toward Dylan's ankle, he cringed at what he saw and realized he'd spoken too soon. A metal rod stuck through the bottom part of Dylan's jeans. And his white sock was stained an unmistakable bright red color. Dylan was bleeding.

CHAPTER 5

Joey wondered if Dylan was in shock. Maybe that was why he didn't seem to be in pain. He gingerly felt around where the metal rod had pierced Dylan's jeans, shining the light from the cell phone so he could see. He let out a sigh of relief. The metal rod had pierced the denim, but it had only grazed Dylan's ankle — he was lucky. "I've solved the mystery of why you can't move," Joey called out to Dylan. "You've got a metal stake that went clean through the bottom of your jeans."

"Well, gosh, pull it out!" Dylan yelled.

"It could be supporting the concrete above in some way." Joey said. "If I loosen it, everything could fall in. We could both be trapped." He paused. "Or worse."

"Maybe you should wiggle out of your jeans," Joey heard Fiona suggest.

"And walk around in my underwear? I don't think so," Dylan said.

"Well, would you rather stay trapped?" Fiona snapped. Joey couldn't blame her for the exasperation in her voice. They were all feeling stressed, on edge.

Joey continued to inspect where the rod

had impaled the denim. "The rod is too close to his ankle," he said. "So there's not enough room for him to get his foot free like that anyway. But if I had something sharp, I could cut him loose. It's only an inch or two from the bottom of his jeans — just a quick slash and he should be able to crawl out. Jeans and all."

"I think I've got a pocketknife," said Dylan. "I just put new grip tape on my skateboard, and I could swear I stashed the knife in my back pocket."

It was getting hot and stuffy under the concrete, and Joey was beginning to feel claustrophobic. He inched his way backward until he could reach Dylan's back pocket, fumbled around until he found the knife, then wiggled himself farther into the cramped space. Going this deep was dangerous, but what else could he do?

Joey set the phone down and carefully opened the pocketknife in the dark. He felt around until his fingers found the rod, and slipped the blade through the hole it made in Dylan's jeans. Then he sawed back and forth through the thick material. It went pretty easily until he reached the hem, which was doubled in thickness. Joey worked as quickly as he could. And it was a good thing, too. At the moment the blade finally sliced through the last threads, the earth began to shake.

"You're free! Get out!" Joey shouted. He felt Dylan scrambling to slip out of the narrow space beside him. Joey tried his best to scooch backward, but it was slower than crawling in had been. He could feel the shuddering ground against his stomach and heard the scraping of concrete in motion just inches from his head.

Suddenly, he felt a tug on his ankles. In one whoosh he was dragged into the open air just as the concrete slabs that had covered him only moments earlier gave way. He closed his eyes as tiny bits and pieces of debris hit his face. A second later the earth was still.

"Who pulled me out?" he asked his friends, their shaky expressions a reflection of how he was feeling as he struggled to his feet.

"We both did," Fiona answered. "I took one ankle and Dylan took the other."

They all stared at the concrete slabs that now lay flat against the ground. No one knew what to say. Finally, Dylan broke the silence. "My phone?"

"I forgot to grab it. Sorry," Joey said, knowing it must be in pieces under the rubble.

He waited for Dylan to say something snarky or call him a name, but Dylan just shrugged and said, "That's okay."

Joey asked, "What about Kevin? He was with you, wasn't he?"

Dylan glanced around behind them. He suddenly looked spooked. "Kevin. Oh, gosh, Kevin. You haven't seen him?"

"No," Fiona said. "We made it to the other side of the highway when the earthquake struck."

Dylan shook his head. "It all happened so quickly. Kevin had just finished filming my kickflip, and we were about to follow you guys underneath the overpass. We tried to turn around and run, but this car down the road a bit slammed on its brakes and the one behind it had to swerve onto the sidewalk. It almost hit us. And it blocked our way back toward the skate park. That's when I fell and everything came down on top of me. I think I heard Kevin calling for me, but I couldn't find my voice to yell back at him. I guess I was in shock or something."

"If you heard Kevin calling for you he must be okay," Joey said.

Dylan looked at the ground and shrugged. All of a sudden it seemed like he was trying hard not to cry. "I don't know. I couldn't tell whether or not his voice was coming from under the rubble. Maybe he was buried, too." His voice sounded kind of muffled. "I mean, I guess he could have been walking around trying to find me —

that's what I was hoping anyway. But, you guys, what if he was calling out to me for help? I'm just not sure. By the time I was able to answer him, I didn't hear him anymore."

CHAPTER 6

"So I guess Kevin could be trapped some-where. Like you were," Joey said.

"He'd have to be close." Fiona put her hands on her hips and squinted, scouring the area for signs of their friend.

As they began to investigate, they looked under smaller pieces of concrete and peeked into the shadows of any open-ing they could find in the rubble. "Kevin!

Kevin!" they shouted, their voices growing desperate.

After a good twenty minutes of looking, hope of finding Kevin began to dim. "If he's buried under here somewhere," Joey said, "he'll need more help than we can give him. What we need is a rescue team to come and lift the rubble. Maybe they can find him. Maybe he's okay." Joey didn't sound very sure of himself.

"You're right. He could be lying in a pocket deep in there somewhere . . . just waiting to be rescued," Fiona said. But she and Dylan seemed discouraged, too. Their shoulders slumped and their brows knitted together with worry.

"It's my fault." Dylan's eyes began to

tear up. "We were right with you guys until Kevin stopped to tape me doing a stupid kickflip. We should have been on the other side with you." He wiped at the corner of his eye. "I'm to blame."

"Come on. You couldn't have known," Fiona said gently. She touched his shoulder. "None of us knew."

Dylan just shrugged and stood staring at the ground.

Suddenly, Fiona began to tear up, too, and Joey felt his face grow hot as he tried not to fall apart at the thought of what could have happened to Kevin.

"So what now?" Dylan took a deep breath and looked up.

"I guess we should head for home," Joey said. "We're the only ones who know where Kevin could be. We can tell his parents so they can get the police to bring a rescue team to help find him."

Joey remembered hearing news stories about earthquakes in other countries. Sometimes people were rescued alive and well, even days after the devastation. He wouldn't give up on his friend yet.

Joey, Dylan, and Fiona made their way around the collapsed overpass and trudged up the grassy hillside so they could head for home. Once at the top they carefully made their way down to the sunny spot by the road that Joey and Fiona had found minutes after the quake. Cars that had been occupied were eerily empty. They'd been abandoned. Now they were just ghosts on a once busy road.

Fiona let out a shriek and pointed into the distance. For a moment Joey held his breath. He couldn't handle any more drama right now. He just couldn't.

But it turned out he didn't have to. Running toward them, with a huge smile on his face, was Kevin!

Fiona and Joey were stunned. It was a miracle! "Dude!" Dylan rushed toward Kevin and threw his arms around their once missing friend, hoisting him up, spinning him around. "You're okay!

You're really okay!" he shouted. Then he plopped Kevin down and shook him to make sure he was real. "Oh, man! I can't believe it!"

Suddenly, Kevin was laughing, and soon Fiona and Joey scrambled over to them, and joined right in.

"Where have you guys been all this time?" Kevin asked.

Joey explained what had happened, and Kevin's eyes grew wide in amazement.

"Ithoughtyouweregoners," Kevin said. He spoke super fast, his adrenaline pumping out of control. "Especially you, Dylan! One moment we were running beside each other and the next everything came crashing down. I tried calling out for you. But when you didn't answer, I figured the worst had happened." He turned to face Joey. "So I started looking for you and Fiona. I knew you were ahead of us and was hoping to find you on the other side of the hill." He gestured to the left.

"We were looking for you and Dylan . . . but went around the other way," Fiona said. "Crazy. We must have just missed each other!"

"Well, I'm glad I finally found you guys," Kevin said. "I was just about to give up and head for home."

"Home! That's where we need to be. Enough talking. Let's get going!" Fiona declared.

The group picked their way over to the sidewalk and started off in the direction of their neighborhood. The path was littered with fallen trees and split by large cracks in the concrete, but it was still the best place to travel on foot.

"Guys, look what I managed to hang on to!" Kevin held up his camcorder and began recording what was once so familiar and now seemed so strange.

Joey had walked along this road a million times. It was so ordinary that he never paid much attention to the orderly buildings and well-kept homes. But now he took in every little detail. It was fascinating and disturbing at the same time. A few lucky houses had miraculously remained standing. In the late-afternoon glow of the setting sun, they looked smug, almost defiant. "Take that, you earthquake!" they seemed to say.

Most, however, were not so lucky. The neighborhood was a total mess.

As Dylan led them toward home, Joey noticed something else. The back pocket of Dylan's jeans hung by a thread and a large gaping rip along the pocket seam exposed his boxers. Joey couldn't believe what he saw:

Tough Guy Dylan was wearing *Star Wars* underwear! If it were any other day, Joey would have laughed. Maybe even pointed it out to everyone. After all the teasing he'd endured, Dylan would have deserved it. But joking around seemed out of place today.

And so they walked in silence.

CHAPTER 7

Away from the collapsed overpass, traffic was beginning to creep along beside the kids. Occasionally an anxious driver, frantic to get home, would honk his horn impatiently. Joey wondered what the honking would accomplish. *Nothing*, he thought. He glanced up at the line of cars every few seconds, hoping to see his father's car. Every time he spotted anything resembling Mr. Flores's gray sedan, his heart jumped. But it sank just as quickly when he'd realize someone else was behind the wheel.

As they trudged along, Joey noticed neighbors congregated in front yards, inspecting the damage to their homes. Their faces lined with grim determination, some had even begun to pick up broken glass, scattered bricks, and pieces of siding. Others, overwhelmed by the sight of the destruction, could do nothing but sob.

BOOM! The sudden sound of an explosion made everyone jump. Joey, Fiona, Dylan, and Kevin exchanged worried looks.

"What the heck was *that*?" Dylan

scrunched up his face. "I know it wasn't an aftershock."

Moments later the wail of sirens could be heard in the distance. It was a reassuring noise, but Joey knew it would be a long while before everyone who needed help would get it.

"I smell gas," Fiona said. "And smoke."

A block later they found the source. A house was burning. Fire leapt from the front window as three kids huddled near their father, and a small concerned crowd gathered around them. A yellow Lab paced back and forth, his barks growing louder by the second. Joey heard someone shout, "Is everyone out?"

"Yes, thank God!" the father yelled.

"We were all outside when the explosion hit — even the dog. Must have been a broken gas line."

The sound of the fire truck's siren grew louder. Cars dutifully pulled over, and soon the wailing noise was ringing in Joey's ears.

Kevin had been filming the whole time, and he zoomed in as the firefighters sprang into action. Joey felt like he was on the set of a blockbuster action movie. One with stuntmen and special effects and professional cameras. *That's how this should be filmed,* he thought. *Not just Kevin using his dinky little camcorder.* None of it seemed real. He wished a director would leap out of nowhere and yell "Cut!"

Joey and his friends left the burning house behind, knowing the firefighters would soon have it under control. But they had only gone about a block when a little girl emerged from behind a large green house with a dark wood door. She ran up to them, her eyes huge with fright. She looked like she was about five years old. Her hair was in messy, lopsided pigtails, her cheeks were wet with tears, and her chest heaved in sobs. "Mommy!" she gasped. "Mommy! I can't find my mommy!"

Fiona knelt down and held the girl's tiny hands. In a calm voice she said, "Do you live around here, sweetie?"

"Yes," the little girl said. She pulled one of her hands away from Fiona and pointed

at the green house with the wood door.
"That's my house."

"What's your name?" Fiona asked.

"Emma. Emma Renee Abernathy." She managed a tiny smile, like she was proud of her name. She had a deep dimple in one cheek, Joey noticed. Just like his sister, Allie.

Fiona smiled back. "I'm Fiona. When did you last see your mom?"

Emma frowned in thought. "I was outside playing in the backyard. Mommy was in the kitchen doing dishes, watching me out the window. She waved to me. Then everything was shaking. The back porch fell! I got scared and hid in my playhouse. I was afraid to come out, so I stayed there a long time." She paused and then added, like it was somehow important, "My playhouse is pink. It has a plastic refrigerator."

"It sounds very nice," Fiona told her.

Joey studied the house the girl had pointed to. It was damaged, but still standing. He wondered if Emma's mother was trapped inside.

"Dylan and I will go inside the house and look for her mom," he told everyone. Dylan was strong, and Joey wasn't sure what they'd find inside the house. He just knew no one should go in there alone. "Kevin and Fiona, you stay with Emma."

As Dylan and Joey approached the house, Joey grew apprehensive. He eyed the partially collapsed roof. What if the house was unstable?

Dylan must have been thinking the same thing. "You sure this is a good idea?" he asked, one eyebrow cocked suspiciously.

"What if it was *your* mom that was trapped inside? Wouldn't you want someone to check on her?" Joey asked.

Dylan simply nodded.

The pair advanced slowly, nervously approaching the front porch. But before they reached the front door, Joey heard a joyful yelp from behind.

"Mommy! Mommy!"

Joey turned in time to see a frantic-looking woman clear across the street. "Emma!" she screamed, bringing her hands to her face in shocked relief. "Oh, thank heavens! Thank heavens!" The only thing stopping Mrs. Abernathy from running into the road and snatching Emma up in a big hug was the slithering sprawl of a downed power line blocking the sidewalk in front of her.

Suddenly, Emma broke away from Fiona's grasp and darted toward her mother.

Later, Joey would say it all happened quickly. And yet, weirdly, everything also seemed to play out in slow motion at the same time.

"Emma! Stop!" Fiona didn't know what to do. "Stop!"

Mrs. Abernathy waved her arms. "No! Emma, no!"

Before Joey knew it he was running harder than he ever had in his entire life. He had to reach Emma before she reached the sidewalk. Because if the little girl touched the downed power line she'd be electrocuted.

CHAPTER 8

Joey raced past Fiona, who by now had also started running after the little girl. But Emma was so excited to see her mom, none of it mattered. She was oblivious to the danger. *She doesn't know any better,* Joey thought as he drew in a ragged breath. *She's just a kid.*

Just as she was within inches of the wire, Joey lurched forward. He snatched her purple T-shirt, jerking her backward, and swooped her into his arms in the nick of time!

The girl struggled, kicking against him. "Put me down! I want my mommy! I want my mommy!" she protested.

But Joey didn't loosen his hold. He slowly inched away from the downed line as Emma's mother rushed halfway down the street and back to avoid it.

When she reached Joey, she took Emma from him, hugging her tightly and burying her face in the little girl's hair. "I couldn't find Emma after the quake. She was there, right outside the window, but I couldn't get the back door open because the porch roof came down. I had to get out through the front door and by the time I ran out to the backyard she was gone! I thought maybe she'd gone across the street to her friend Jessica's house. But when she wasn't there, I ran around the neighborhood from house to house looking for her." She kissed her daughter's cheek. "Oh, Emma! Where on earth were you?"

"In the playhouse," Emma mumbled. She nuzzled into her mother's neck.

"The playhouse?" Her mother started to laugh. "The playhouse?"

"I was scared," Emma said.

"Oh, baby, I was scared, too."

By this time Fiona, Dylan, and Kevin had walked over to where they were standing.

Mrs. Abernathy stared at the downed power line. "You saved my daughter," she told Joey. "You saved Emma's life. If you hadn't reached her in time . . ." Her voice trailed off and she shook her head at the thought. "How can I ever thank you?"

Joey didn't know what to say. He just shrugged. "I'm just glad she is okay."

"Do you run track at school?" the woman asked. "I don't think I've ever seen anyone run that fast!"

"No. Just pure adrenaline, I guess," Joey said as Emma looked up and gave him a shy, one-dimpled smile. She seemed to have forgiven him for grabbing her. "I've got a little sister at home," Joey said. "Emma reminds me of her."

"Well, she's very lucky to have you as a brother."

Joey thought about how frustrated he was with Allie when he last saw her at the skate park. He wasn't so sure she really was lucky to have him. But he'd change that. If only he found her safe and sound once he made it home, he'd try to be the best big brother ever.

"We'd better get going," Fiona said.

"Thanks again," Mrs. Abernathy said to Joey. She frowned. "I don't even know your name . . ."

"Joey Flores."

"Well, Joey Flores, you're a hero!" She smiled.

With that, the group waved good-bye and continued on. No one said a word. It had been a long day.

They hadn't gone more than half a block when Fiona broke the silence. "Joey, you saved my life, too."

"What are you talking about?" he asked, looking at her sideways.

"When the earthquake struck and we were under the overpass, I froze in my tracks. I was so surprised, I couldn't move. I couldn't even think. It was like I was paralyzed — my brain, my arms and legs. Just everything! You could have bolted.

But you didn't. You pulled me and dragged me until something kicked in and I began to move. If you had run off without me, I wouldn't have made it out. I would've been buried."

Again, Joey didn't know how to respond. He knew what Fiona was saying was true. But he just felt grateful to have his friend walking by his side. He didn't feel like a hero. Heroes were larger than life. He was just ten-year-old Joey. "You would have done the same for me. If I'd frozen, too, you probably would have come to your senses and dragged me out as well."

"Well, I'm glad we didn't have to find out!"

Joey shrugged and grinned. "Me, too."

"Joey?" Dylan said.

"Yeah?"

Dylan stared ahead, not really looking at him. "You . . . you kind of . . . sort of . . ." He stumbled over the words and then suddenly reached over and punched his arm. "You saved me, too, buddy. I mean, you were the one who figured out why I was stuck. You crawled into that tiny space and cut me loose. I would've been crushed in that aftershock. If you hadn't made it out, too, I never would have forgiven myself. It would've been all my fault."

"But I did make it out. You made sure of that. Remember?" Joey told him.

"Well, let's just say I owe you. Big-time. Okay? I'd be a pancake right now if not for you."

It occurred to Joey that since the quake, Dylan had not teased him. Not even once. Joey grinned and couldn't resist saying, "Okay. You owe me. Big-time."

Dylan punched him again. "You're all right, for a little dude."

Joey punched him back. "Gee, thanks."

"Oh, shoot!" Kevin exclaimed.

"What?" everyone asked at once.

"The battery on my camcorder just died. And I didn't get that touching moment — or Dylan's IOU — recorded."

"Well, thank goodness for that!" Dylan said, and they all laughed.

But the kids soon grew quiet as they neared their homes. Joey thought of the happy, joyful reunion little Emma had with her mother. Would he be as lucky? Would Kevin, Fiona, and Dylan?

"Well, I guess this is me," said Fiona as they approached her street. She gave her friends a nervous wave. "See you guys later." She turned and headed off toward her house. Soon it was Kevin's turn to say good-bye. Joey and Dylan walked in silence toward their apartment building. Who knew what they would find when they arrived?

CHAPTER 9

Now Joey and Dylan were only about a block from their apartment building. With each step Joey grew more anxious and scared. His heart thumped. He was aware of each and every beat.

Dylan stared straight ahead, but he reached over and thumped Joey on the back reassuringly. "Almost there, bro."

Joey nodded. They passed by an

emergency squad parked outside a heavily damaged building. An EMT wheeled a woman toward the ambulance on a stretcher. She had a neck brace on and her head was bandaged, but she was conscious.

Grand old trees lined the streets. This was a historic part of the city — Joey's mother and father loved the quaint, well-kept looks of the neighborhood and the architecture. But it didn't look well kept anymore. A few of the trees had been uprooted by the power of the quake. One had crashed into the roof of a house. Another sprawled across the sidewalk and blocked one lane of traffic.

Joey squinted. He should be able to see

the roof of their apartment complex on the horizon. It was several stories taller than the single-family homes and other smaller apartment buildings nearby. Unless . . . unless it had collapsed. His throat grew tight. He clenched his fists and told himself to breathe.

Finally he caught a glimpse of the roof above the tree line! The building was still standing, but he could see that some of the support beams under the roof were exposed. That couldn't be good. He quickened his pace, breaking into a jog, then a full-out run. Dylan followed suit.

By the time they reached the complex they were nearly breathless. They were greeted by broken windows, lopsided balconies, and scattered pieces of debris. Part of an outer wall had fallen and Joey could see tumbled beds, refrigerators, tables, and chairs inside two apartments. It was like looking into a gigantic dollhouse. In one apartment the furniture looked especially familiar. He gasped. It was Dylan's apartment. The one he shared with his mother and grandmother.

"No!" Dylan said.

They both started toward the entrance door, but were stopped by a policeman before they could get too close. "Sorry, boys," he said. "This structure hasn't been declared safe yet."

"But my mother and sister are in there!" Joey said. "I have to see them!"

"The building has been evacuated. There's no one left inside."

"Is everyone okay?" Dylan asked.

The policeman just shrugged and shook his head.

An ambulance screamed down the

street. Was it carrying someone Joey knew? His sister? His mom?

"Most of the residents have gathered on the basketball courts behind the building for now. Why don't you check there," the policeman said. "If you can't find your families, come back and let me know."

Joey and Dylan hightailed it to the basketball courts. The space was full of people milling about. Joey rushed into the crowd, weaving his way back and forth, eyes darting in every direction.

Finally he spied his mom. She was holding Allie and talking to the elderly man who lived in the apartment across from theirs. She looked tired, and even from across the court, Joey could see her

glistening, bloodshot eyes. "Mom!" he
called out.

She turned and ran toward him, balanc-
ing Allie on one hip. As soon as they
reached each other, his mother hugged him
close. "Thank God you're okay." She kept

saying it over and over again as she clung to him. "Thank God you're okay. Thank God you're okay."

"Dad?" Joey asked. "What about Dad? Where is he? Have you heard from him?"

She squinted with worry. "Not yet." She smiled in an attempt to be reassuring. "He's probably stuck in traffic — it's crazy out there. There must be lots of detours slowing things down. It could be a while before he makes it to us, but I'm sure he's fine."

A rush of emotions hit so heavy and deep, it caught Joey off guard. He was relieved to find his mom and Allie, but worried about his dad. He sank down onto the asphalt of the basketball court and rested his head on his knees for a moment. When he looked up he saw Dylan, just yards from where he sat. Dylan's grandmother had cupped her grandson's face in her hands and she was smothering him with kisses, while his mom wiped tears from her eyes. Dylan didn't look like he minded too much. He glanced over at Joey and rolled his eyes, but he was grinning.

Suddenly, a man in a suit was clapping his hands and whistling for everyone's attention. "I need you to gather around," he shouted. "I'm from the department of building and safety, and I have an announcement to make."

Everyone scurried to find a place where they would be able to hear whatever news the official had to say. Joey stayed close to his mother's side as they made their way toward the front of the crowd.

After everyone settled down, the man began to speak. "No one will be permitted to enter any of the apartments in this complex tonight."

CHAPTER 10

The crowd erupted in frustrated groans.

The man put his hands up. "I know this isn't the news you wanted to hear, but we can't let you into the building until it passes a safety inspection. Besides the obvious repairs to the outer wall, we need to make sure the structure is sound. There may be further damage we can't see and we need experts to come in and take a look."

"So when will that be? When can we go back to our homes?" someone asked.

"I can't say for sure. But please know the city will be working overtime to get things back to normal as quickly as possible. In the meantime, if you need a place to stay, the recreation center on Quinton Street is being set up to handle emergency accommodations."

"So what are we going to do?" Joey asked his mother.

"I guess we should head for the recreation center," she said.

"But what about Dad?" Joey couldn't help but ask.

Mrs. Flores put her arm around him. "Don't worry. He'll find us."

But Joey did worry. He wouldn't be able to relax until his family was back together again.

Some of Joey's neighbors decided to stay with relatives or friends, but others had no choice but to camp out at the community recreation center.

Joey, his mother, and Allie were greeted by Red Cross volunteers, who took down their names and information. This made Joey feel a tiny bit better. Perhaps this could help his father track them down. That was, *if* he was okay.

Cots lined the gym. Donated sandwiches and bottles of water were handed out. The air was warm and people fanned themselves to stay cool in the cramped conditions. But even though it wasn't a swanky hotel, nobody seemed to care. They were too busy swapping stories. Everyone was just happy to have survived the quake.

After scarfing down a ham and cheese sandwich, Joey set up camp on one of the cots. Mrs. Flores sat at a folding table, talking to their neighbors while she tried to entertain Allie. Things were so hectic and confusing that Joey hadn't had a chance to tell her exactly what he'd been through. But maybe that was for the best. He had a feeling she'd totally freak out if she knew.

Joey sighed. A long evening lay ahead with nothing much to do. After a while,

Dylan came over with a deck of cards and sat next to him. "A lady was passing these out," he said. "You want to play a game of rummy?"

"Sure," Joey said. But it was hard to concentrate on the game with his father missing. He tried not to think about the cars he'd seen — the ones crumpled and crushed by the overpass — but the images wouldn't leave him alone.

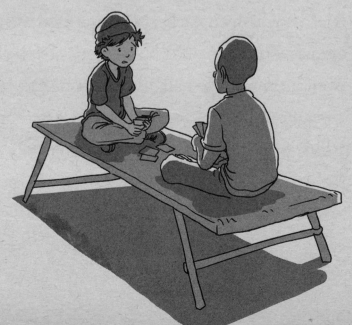

"I wonder how Kevin and Fiona are doing," Joey said more to himself than to Dylan.

But Dylan nodded. "I'd call them, but my phone . . . well, you know." As he trailed off, Joey realized that the earthquake had really shaken everything up. The outside world and the one inside each of them. He hoped his friends were okay. That their houses weren't flattened like some of the ones they'd seen earlier. He squinted at his cards, as if that would help erase the images from his mind. He had a seven of hearts and an eight of hearts, and Dylan just discarded a nine of hearts. He picked it up and placed the sequence of cards face up on the cot, when Dylan suddenly poked him.

"What?" Joey protested. "That was a legit move."

Dylan just grinned and pointed behind Joey.

Joey turned around to find his father pushing through the gym doors. He looked tired and stressed, his dress shirt unbuttoned and his tie undone. But when he saw Joey, his whole face brightened. Joey didn't care who was watching, he jumped up and ran into his father's outstretched arms.

"Hey there, Joey!" His father hugged him close. "Where's your mom and Allie?"

"Over at the tables." Joey pointed. He'd never felt this excited in his life! Not on Christmas morning, not on the day he'd gotten his skateboard. Absolutely nothing compared to this. He had his family. *We're together and that's all that really matters,* he thought as he and his dad made their way over to the table. His mom must have agreed because now the entire Flores family was wrapped in one giant hug.

"What a drive home!" his father said, once the ecstatic reunion was over. "Some major roads were closed. It was stop and go most of the way. I heard the old Franklin Street overpass collapsed."

"It did," Joey said. His parents looked at

him in surprise. He explained how he was under the overpass when the quake struck. That he and Fiona had narrowly escaped and how they'd rescued Dylan and found Kevin. His mother's eyes were about to bug out of her head, and instantly Joey regretted shooting off his mouth about what had happened. She'd probably never let him walk to or from the skate park on his own again.

But maybe he didn't know his mother as well as he thought. "It sounds like you knew exactly what you needed to do to keep yourself and your friends safe. I'm proud of you," she said.

"I am, too," his father said, ruffling his hair. "I'm glad you're my son."

"I'm glad you're my dad," Joey said, and he really truly meant it with all his heart.

Later that evening, Joey and Dylan continued their game of rummy and played a few more rounds. But it was still hard for Joey to focus on the game and he ended up losing big. He had a happy ending with his family, and Dylan did, too. But what about Fiona and Kevin? Were their homes destroyed? Were their families okay? The answers to those questions remained a mystery.

CHAPTER 11

Two weeks later, Joey had all the answers he wanted. He, Fiona, Kevin, and Dylan were gathered around a laptop in Joey's room. Kevin was finally going to upload the video he had shot at the skate park so they could see it.

Things were just beginning to return to normal. Joey's and Dylan's families had to stay at the recreation center for nearly a week before their building was declared safe to return to. It had seemed sort of like camping out at first, but everyone quickly grew tired of the overcrowded conditions, prepackaged food, and stiff cots.

When Joey finally stepped inside the Flores's apartment he felt like he might burst with happiness. Sure, the place was a bit dusty and stuffy, but aside from a few fallen items, it looked exactly like they had just left for a quick outing. A few of Allie's toys lay scattered on the living room floor and some dirty dishes waited in the sink — there hadn't been time to pick up after the quake struck. But to Joey, there was no place he'd rather be. This was home and he had missed its comforts.

Kevin connected his camcorder to Joey's laptop and double-clicked on the movie-app icon.

"How's your dad doing?" Joey asked. Kevin's father had been at work when the quake struck and a wall had fallen in on top of him. He had some internal injuries and spent a few days at the hospital.

Kevin smiled. "Great. Thanks. He's back at work now. Almost fully recovered."

"I'm glad," said Joey. And for the millionth time since the earthquake struck, he really was. Everyone else in Kevin's family made it through okay — and Fiona's family, too. Joey knew he and his friends had been very lucky.

"Here we go!" Kevin said. All at once,

the noise of the skate park filled the room — the clatters, the clanks, kids talking and yelling.

There was Joey and his slick rail slide, pumping his fist in the air when he landed. Then Fiona swooped down the half-pipe effortlessly just before the screen cut to Joey dropping in for the first time. It showed him falling halfway down with a sheepish look, and later, grinning with success.

Seeing his skateboard made Joey a little sad. He'd lost it in the quake. But he knew one day he'd get another one, that he'd enjoy hanging at the skate park with his friends again.

The group watched intently — their eyes glued to the laptop screen — when the scenery suddenly changed. Instead of the skate park there was a quick image of the overpass ahead and then a close-up of Dylan doing his kickflip. The shot was taken only moments before the world had gone mad.

They solemnly watched what Kevin had documented: the mountain of concrete from the collapsed overpass, homes and buildings utterly destroyed, people in shock, neighbors helping one another. They saw the horrible glow of the house on fire and felt relief all over again when the fire truck showed up. Then came a clip of little Emma waving good-bye to them from the safety of her mother's arms.

Joey thought of his own family. How annoyed he'd always get with his parents and Allie, and how, since the quake, he had grown to appreciate them more. How he'd wanted a cooler dad, but was now so grateful to just have a happy, healthy one who loved him. He knew his family would manage to annoy him again from time to time. That was inevitable. But he'd never look at things exactly the same way again. He would never take his family or friends for granted. The earth had shifted, but so had his perspective about things.

Suddenly, the video cut to a close-up of . . . Dylan's ripped back pocket seam. And there amid the sadness and destruction and generosity and hope of that day were C-3PO and R2-D2 peeking out of the large tear in Dylan's jeans.

"What the heck?" Dylan exclaimed. "Kevin, I'm going to get you for this!" Everyone laughed, including Dylan. He gave a sheepish shrug and said, "Hey, there's nothing wrong with *Star Wars*. It's a classic, you know."

If Dylan ever gave him a hard time in

the future, Joey figured at least he'd have an embarrassing story about him to share now. But somehow he thought, with all that had happened, Dylan wouldn't be much of a problem anymore.

More About
EARTHQUAKES

More than 500,000 earthquakes strike all over the world every year. Scientists use machines called seismometers to measure the magnitude, or size and intensity, of earthquakes. An earthquake with a magnitude of 3 or under usually can't be felt, but anything over a magnitude 6 has the potential to cause serious damage.

The outside crust of the earth is made of large pieces — or plates — that move slowly. When these plates collide or rub against each other, they can trigger an earthquake. And when a quake cracks the earth's crust and causes violent shaking, highways may collapse and buildings can be destroyed.

While the shaking ground is dangerous, earthquakes can cause other natural disasters such as avalanches and landslides that can be even more deadly. Undersea earthquakes can trigger tsunamis, or giant waves, that can flood the coasts.

San Francisco, California, suffered a major earthquake on April 18, 1906. The quake lasted only a minute, but it ignited fires that burned through the city for three days, and destroyed around 490 city blocks.

More recently, a quake hit Indonesia on December 26, 2004. This earthquake lasted nearly ten minutes — the longest earthquake on record.

On January 12, 2010, an earthquake hit the island of Haiti. Around 3.5 million people were affected by the disaster, and 4,000 schools were damaged or destroyed.

In the United States, Alaska has the most earthquakes of any state, but California's earthquakes do the most damage.

Some scientists have observed animals acting strangely before a quake. Frogs and bees have been known to leave their homes, and chickens have refused to lay eggs! No one knows how or why animals sense the oncoming quake.

Earthquakes are very hard to predict. If you feel the ground begin to shake, here are a few things you can do to help keep yourself safe:

- Stay away from windows and heavy furniture like bookcases or dressers that could tip over and trap you.

- Crawling under a table, bed, or desk can also protect you from falling objects.

- If you are outside, try to stand in an open space, far from buildings, trees, or power lines.

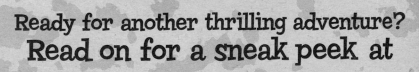

Ready for another thrilling adventure?
Read on for a sneak peek at

TORNADO ALLEY...

By the time they got within a hundred feet of the barn, rain cut loose from the heavy cloud wall and began to pelt them. Each drop stung Wyatt's face. Alison shrieked like it was great fun riding in the rain. An adventure. Joshua and Jackson laughed, too. But Wyatt didn't appreciate getting soaked to the bone. The air had turned cold, and as the wind started to pick up, he shivered and hustled toward the barn, where he jumped off Licorice and opened the door, letting everyone inside.

They took the tack off the horses and put their gear away, then rubbed and brushed the horses down before leading them into their stalls. Duncan trotted off to check on his goats, with Alison close behind. She climbed into the pen, scratched the mama goat under her chin, then picked up one of her tiny week-old triplet babies and nuzzled it with her cheek. "You are sooooo sweet," she said. "I wish I could take you home with me."

Duncan barked.

"Oh, and you, too, Duncan!" Alison laughed. "I would probably have better luck bringing a pygmy goat into the apartment than Duncan," she called to the boys. "I can't believe how small these goats are. Even the mama. Duncan is way bigger!"

Just as Joshua and Jackson were about to climb into the goat pen with Alison, Wyatt turned to them and frowned.

"We should go inside," he said. He

wanted to change into some dry clothes and play video games with Joshua and Jackson before they had to go home. But all at once an ear-shattering clatter shook the metal roof of the barn.

The kids all jumped in surprise.

Hail? Wyatt wondered. He peeked out the barn door while the others scrambled over the rails of the goat pen after him. Hail stones about the size of golf balls bounced off the ground.

"Holy cow!" Jackson said.

"Oh my gosh!" Alison stood with her mouth gaping open.

Joshua stuck his hand outside, like he wanted to catch a piece of hail. Jackson quickly pulled his younger brother back.

"Don't be stupid. That hail is big enough to hurt you!"

Then just as suddenly as the hail started, it stopped.

"Man, that was weird!" Joshua said.

As the kids walked toward the house, the air felt oddly still. Quiet. It was unsettling. Especially after the driving rain and hail they'd just experienced.

Wyatt looked westward, the direction the storm had come from, and saw something so surreal and terrifying on the horizon that he had to do a double take to make sure his eyes weren't deceiving him. For a moment he stood absolutely still, awestruck by the enormous funnel cloud that kicked up swirling columns of dust in the distance. There was something hypnotizing about it. Part of Wyatt wanted to stand there and watch, but soon his common sense took over.

"Tornado!" Wyatt screamed. "Get to the storm shelter!" He pointed at the cellar doors by the side of the house. "We have to get to shelter. Run!"

For a split second, the others froze in their tracks, startled by Wyatt's outburst, until they, too, saw the tornado. The wind picked up and whipped around them, pushing away the stillness, and all four kids bolted, making a beeline for safety.

Wyatt was surprised to see Alison outrun them all. She was fast and reached the cellar doors first, quickly followed by long-legged Jackson. They heaved open the doors, revealing a staircase down to the cellar, and paused for a moment, waiting for Wyatt and Joshua to catch up.

"Don't wait. Get inside!" Wyatt yelled.

Jackson and Alison obeyed his command and disappeared down the steps, with Joshua scrambling in close behind them. *Phew! We're all safe,* Wyatt thought as he darted down the first few steps and reached to close the doors. But before he could get a hold of them, a flash of pink streaked by.

"Duncan is in the barn," Alison shouted as she rushed back up the steps. "I have to go get him and bring him to the cellar!"

"Are you nuts? Get back here!" Wyatt

lunged for her, but she slipped out of his grasp. "There's no time!" he yelled after her with desperation and fury in his voice.

Alison turned and looked at him briefly with panicked eyes. The wind flung her long dark hair every which way. And then in a flash she was gone. Running away from them. Away from safety.

And into the path of a monster.

ABOUT THE AUTHOR

Marlane Kennedy is the author of *Me and the Pumpkin Queen* and *The Dog Days of Charlotte Hayes*. She has lived through one tiny earthquake, the blizzard of 1978, and a tornado that swept through Wooster, Ohio, where she lives with her husband and daughter. Though she is having a blast writing about disasters, she is hoping not to add any more to this list! You can find her online at www.marlanekennedy.com.

MORE FROM ADAM BLADE

DIVE DEEP INTO
ANOTHER ADVENTURE!

BEASTQUEST®

⇥ THE DARK REALM ⇤

FIGHT THE BEASTS

FEAR THE MAGIC